# The Wriggling Snake

Written by Wang Yimei

Illustrated by Zhou You

CARDINAL MEDIA

Something wriggled and twisted and scared the ostriches. What could it be?

Feathers fell as birds scattered.
What could it be?

It was a snake!

The snake liked to
wriggle and twist.
He slithered and slid
anywhere he wanted to go.

But the snake was lonely.
All the other animals
were afraid of him.

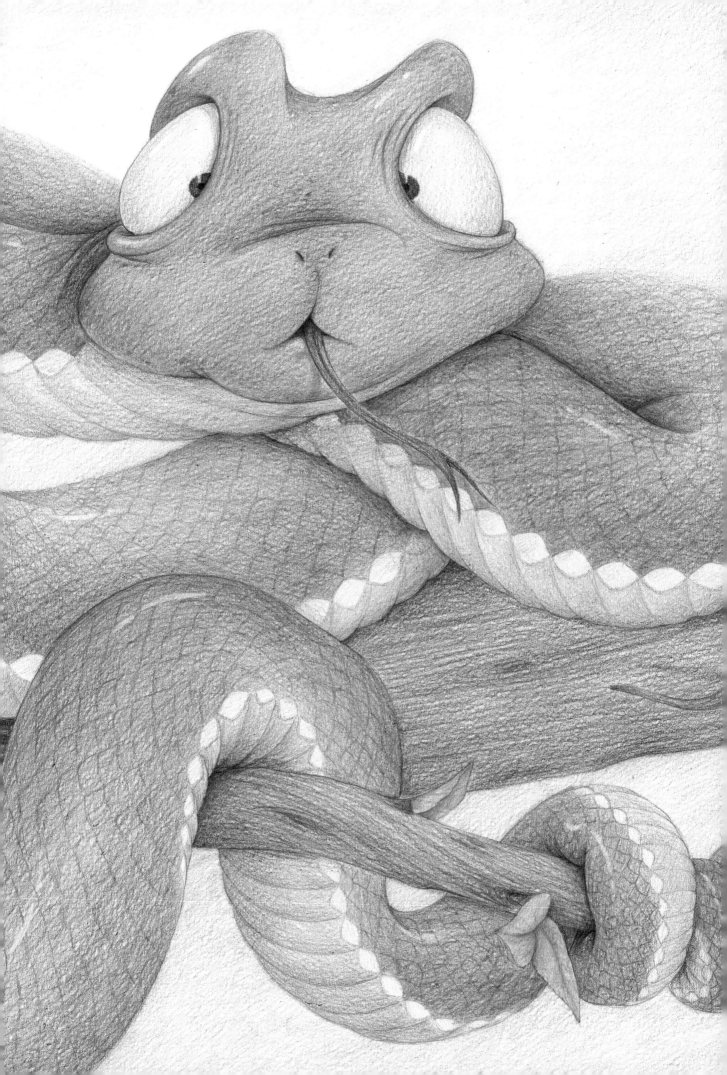

One day the snake met a boy with a flute.
The boy's name was Eli. He was not afraid
of the snake.

The sound of Eli's flute rose and fell. The snake wriggled and twisted along with his music. Together they felt like everything was just right.

Eli and the snake
came to the city square.
Eli played his flute as the snake
performed his twisting dance.

Crowds would pay to see their performance, and Eli grew rich. He bought a house and made lots of new friends.

They were all afraid of the snake.

Eli stopped playing his
flute for the crowds and
ignored the snake.

The snake slithered under the floorboards.

"I'll live quietly under the floor," the snake said,
"but I hope Eli will still play the flute for me."

Eli did play his flute—for his girlfriend. And they were happy together.

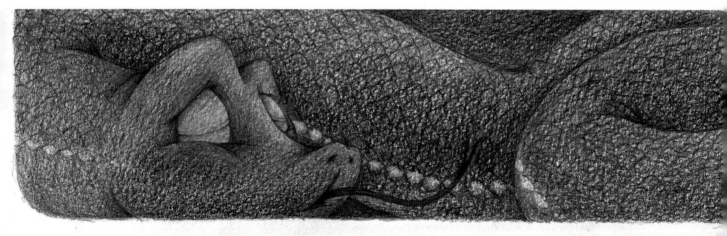

The snake tried to dance but the space under the floor was too small.

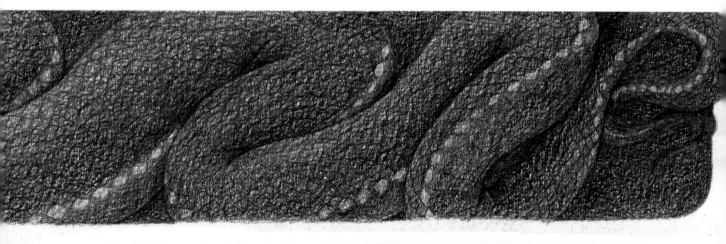

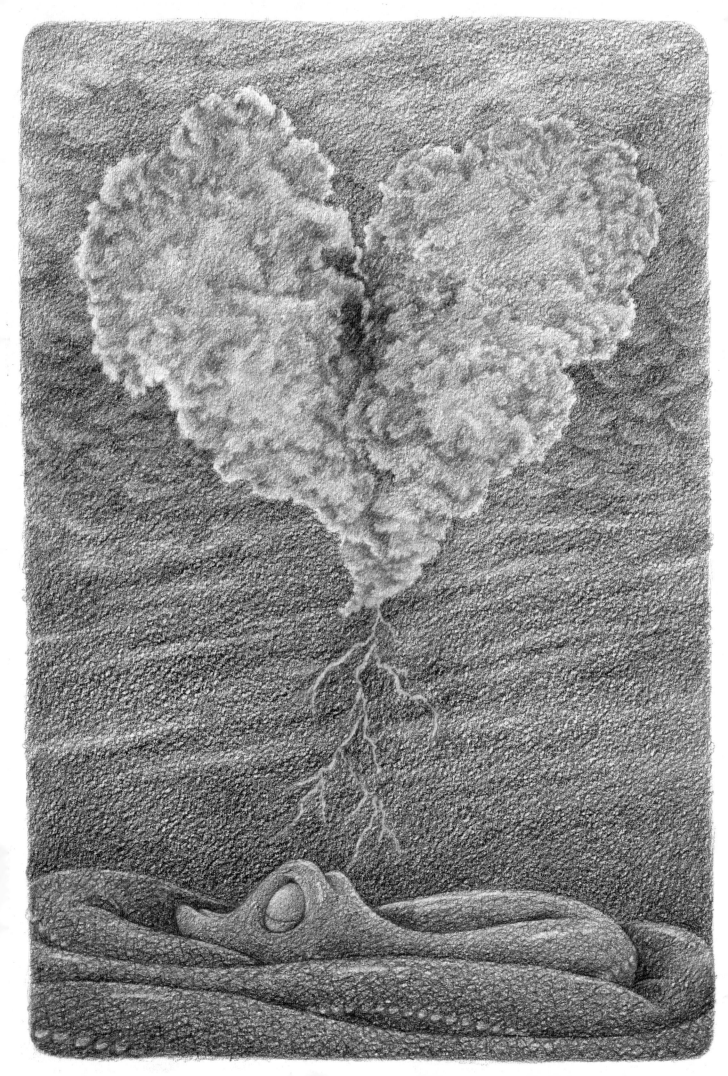

Then the snake stopped hearing the flute.

Instead he heard the sound of angry voices and shouting above his head.

The snake was very lonely and sad. Finally he decided to leave the space under the floor.

The snake went back
to the forest. All the
animals came out
to welcome him.

Now that the snake was a famous performer,
they wanted to see him dance.

Alone in the night, the snake wriggled and twisted.
He coiled into a question mark. "Why?" he asked.

"Why do I miss the boy and his flute so much?"

Time passed.
Eli spent all of his
money and found
himself alone. He had to sell his
furniture, his car, and his house.

But he returned
for one last thing.
What could it be?

His flute! It was hanging on the wall. He picked it up, and then he remembered the snake.

He pressed his ear down to the floor. He listened for sounds of dancing, but he only heard the quiet of the empty house.

Eli walked to the city square
and played a song on his flute.

No one stopped to listen.

Far away in the forest, the snake heard a sound on the wind. What could it be?

The snake began to wriggle and twist toward the music, but he was old and his twisting was slow.

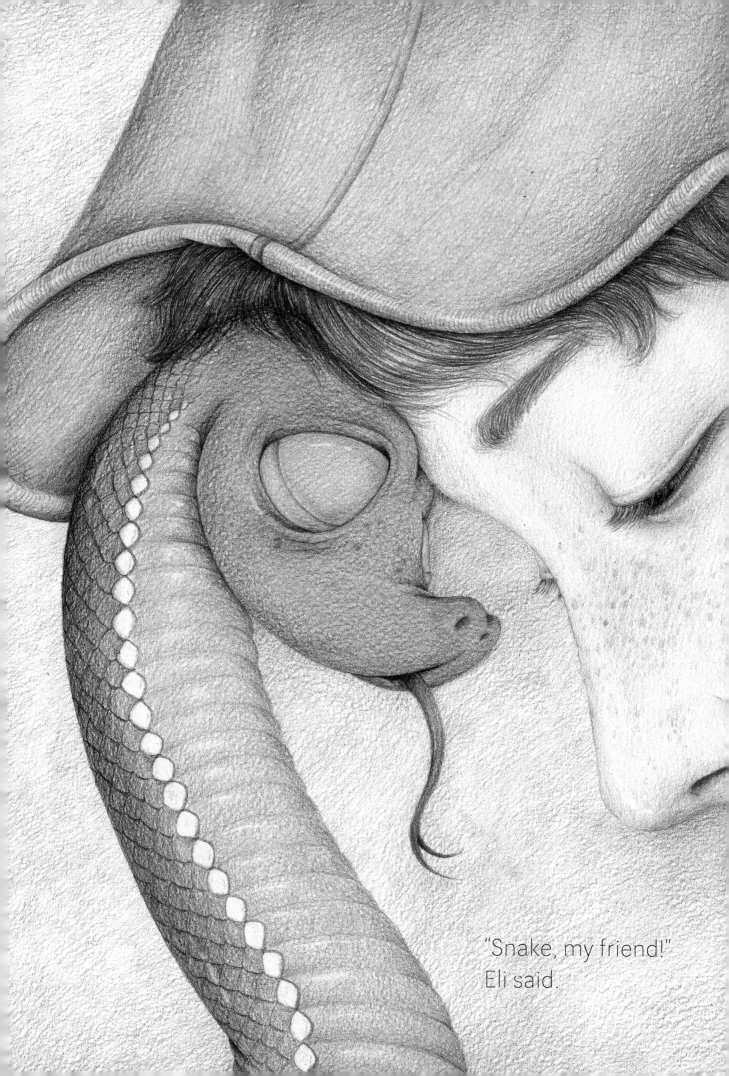

"Snake, my friend!"
Eli said.

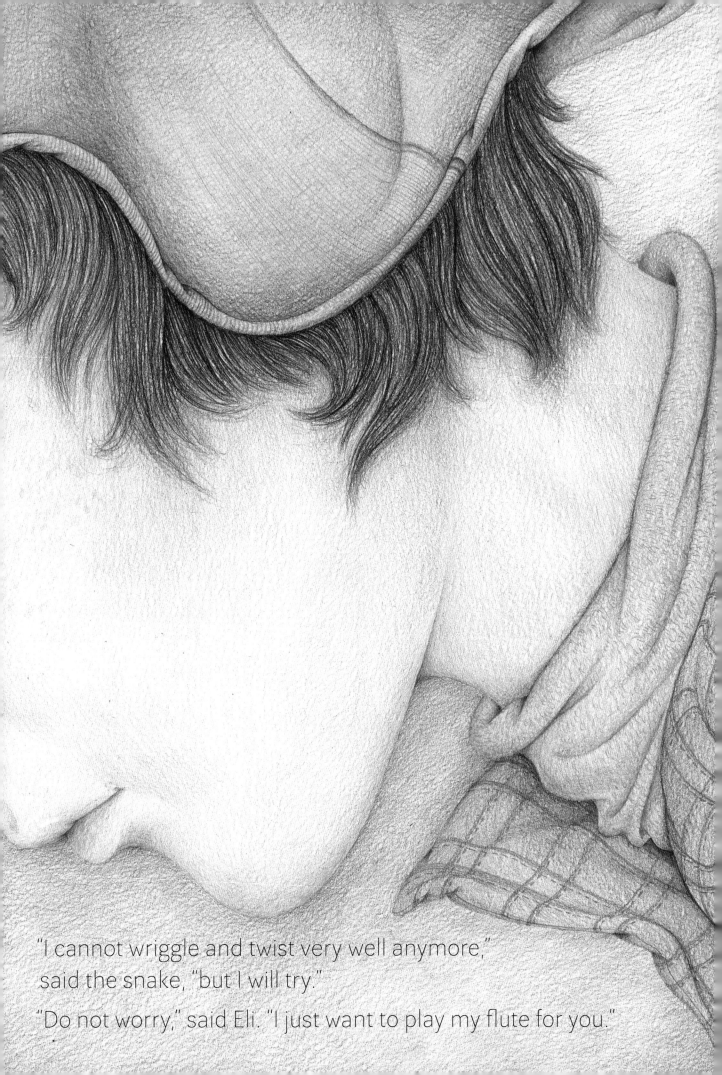

"I cannot wriggle and twist very well anymore,"
said the snake, "but I will try."

"Do not worry," said Eli. "I just want to play my flute for you."

Eli and the snake grew old together.

No crowds gathered to hear a man play the flute and see a snake wriggle and twist.

But Eli and the snake did not care. Together they felt like everything was just right.

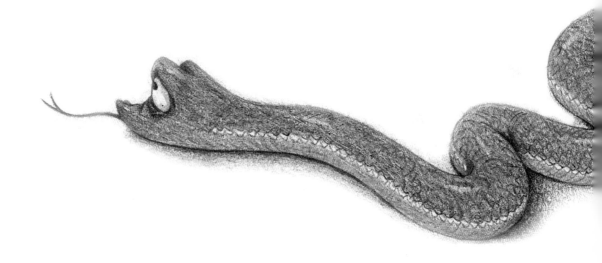